Let's go into the jungle

Rod Campbell

This way to Jungle →

Shhhhh!

Let's go into the jungle
and see who's there today.
We must be very quiet
or the animals will run away!

Shhhhh!

This way
to Jungle →

Grrrrr!

I'm a noisy lion,
all day I growl and roar.
At night I'm noisy too,
that's because I snore!

Grrrrr!

Blaaaaah!

I have two tusks,
my nose is long,
I'm an elephant -
big and strong!

Blaaaaah!

6

Tee, hee, hee!

Ha, ha, ha,
hee, hee, hee!
I'm a monkey
in a tree.
I see you,
can you see me?
Ha, ha, ha,
hee, hee, hee!

Tee, hee, hee!

8

Hisssss!

Stay where you are,
I'm a very shy snake.
To take a step forward
would be a mistake.
If you come any closer
you'd better beware.
I'll drop on your head
and wriggle in your hair!

Hisssss!

Grrrrr!

Tigers are fierce,
tigers can bite.
Tigers can eat you -
if you're naughty
I might!

Grrrrr!

Yawn, yawn!

It's my birthday today,
such a lot of fuss.
Three cheers for me -
hip, hip, hippopotamus!

Yawn, yawn!

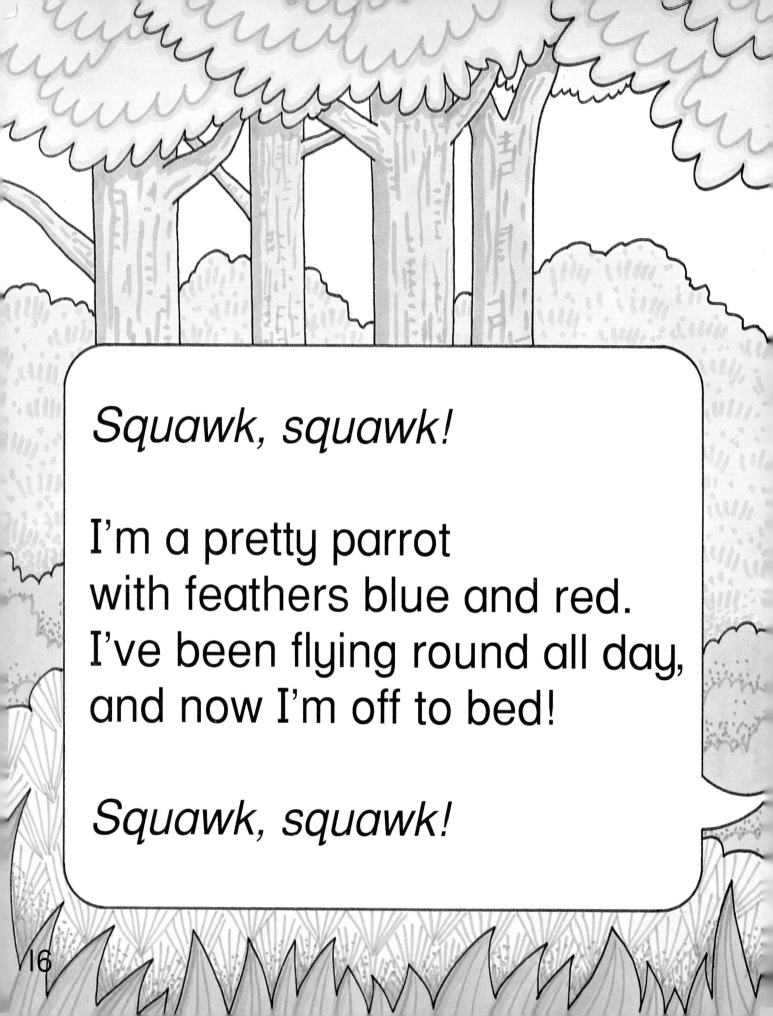

Squawk, squawk!

I'm a pretty parrot
with feathers blue and red.
I've been flying round all day,
and now I'm off to bed!

Squawk, squawk!

17

Mmmmmm!

Yummy, yummy, yummy,
a bear loves honey.
I like it best
when it's in my tummy!
- don't you?

Mmmmmm!

Snap, snap!

I like to smile,
come closer and see.
I'm a crocodile
and I'll eat you for tea!

Snap, snap!

20

22

Will you be our friend
and come and see us soon?
You'll find us in the jungle,
every morning and afternoon.

Bye, bye!

Way out
of Jungle →

23